Sophie and the New Baby

Pictures by Catherine Anholt
Story by Laurence Anholt

Albert Whitman & Company
Morton Grove, Illinois

For Joan, with much love

Library of Congress Cataloging-in-Publication Data
Anholt, Laurence.
Sophie and the new baby / pictures by Catherine Anholt; story by Laurence Anholt.
p.   cm.
Summary: Sophie waits through the seasons of the year for her sibling to be born and then
experiences mixed feelings about the new baby.
ISBN 0-8075-7550-X
[1. Babies—Fiction. 2. Brothers and sisters—Fiction. 3. Seasons—Fiction.]
I. Anholt, Catherine, ill.   II. Title.
PZ7.A5863 So 2000   [E]—dc21   99-050901

Originally published in the United Kingdom by Orchard Books,
an imprint of the Watts Publishing Group, London.

The very first flower pushed its way through the melting snow.
Sophie ran to look, then carefully lifted her rag doll from the carriage.
"Look," she told her, "Spring is here."

Sophie and her mom and dad walked farther into the woods. After a while, Sophie's mom told her a secret. A BIG, IMPORTANT secret.

"Guess what, Sophie?" she said. "Soon you'll have a real little person to play with. We're going to have a new baby. What do you think of that?"

"Will it be at home when we get back?" asked Sophie.
Her dad laughed. "No," he said. "We'll have to wait until the winter.
It will be a Winter Baby."

All through the summer, Sophie waited for the new baby.

In the hot evenings, she took her doll to bed and gave it the best place on her pillow. "You'll have to move over," she told the other toys. "Someone important is coming soon."

Sophie had never waited so long for anything. Sometimes she forgot all about the Winter Baby.

One day, a big brown leaf floated down from the golden trees. Sophie ran to catch it. The leaf drifted slowly from side to side, then it landed gently in the carriage, right next to Sophie's doll.

Her dad smiled. "Now it's Autumn," he said. "The baby will be here soon."

Sophie helped her mom get the baby's room ready. Her dad brought down a little crib that used to be Sophie's, but Sophie was far too big for it now. Next to the crib she made a bed for her own rag doll.

The afternoons were dark. Sophie and her dad played indoors.
Outside, the bare branches were white with frost. Sophie dressed her
doll in warm clothes and carried it carefully, just like a real baby.

Very late one night, Sophie sat up in bed.
Something was different.
Something was coming.

"Why is everything so quiet?"
Sophie asked her doll.
She tiptoed downstairs.

Her dad was looking out the window.

He put his arm around her. "Look, Sophie," he whispered. "It's going to snow."

Sophie looked out at the moonlight. She saw the very first snowflake floating slowly out of the silent sky.

Sophie wished she could stay like that forever. Just her and her dad, watching the world turn white.

That night her brother was born.

At first the baby slept all day. His face was wrinkled, as if he'd been in the bath too long. Sometimes he yawned a huge yawn. Then Sophie leaned over and kissed him. She smelled his special new baby smell and stroked his soft, warm face.

But on other days, her brother cried. He waved his little hands
in the air and yelled. Sophie brought him all her toys and she
even showed him the rag doll, but he wasn't interested.

He wanted to be fed, he wanted to be changed, he wanted to
be cuddled, and he wanted it all *right now.*

"When will he be going back again?" Sophie asked her mom.
Sophie's mom laughed. "This baby isn't going back," she said.
"He's here forever. We can't just put him away like your rag doll."

Sophie wanted someone to play with her in the snow or walk with her in the woods, but her mom and dad were too busy with the baby.

Sophie pointed at her brother. "You said he could play with me," she said.

"You'll have to wait awhile, Sophie," said her dad. "He's not big enough yet."

"I ALWAYS have to wait!" shouted Sophie.

So she took her doll and went out by herself, slamming the door behind her.

The yard was quiet and empty. Sophie bent down and began to play sadly by herself.

The sky turned gray, and the snow fell faster and faster around her.

"You're all alone and cold," she told her snowman, "just like me."

Sophie began to cry. Her tears splashed onto the snow. She looked up at the house where the windows were bright.

Inside, her mom and dad were smiling down at the new baby.

Sophie threw down her rag doll and shouted at the sky ...

I DON'T WANT THAT BABY ANYMORE!"

She cried so much she didn't see her dad coming across the yard.
He lifted her up in his big arms and held her close.
"I know it's hard, Sophie," he said. "Everything's changed for you."

In the kitchen, Sophie's mom made her a warm drink.
"Did you lose your doll?" she asked.
"Yes," sniffed Sophie. "And I don't care."
The rag doll lay forgotten in the snow.

A long time passed before Sophie got used to the Winter Baby. He
began to make little happy noises when he saw Sophie and held tightly
to her finger. And then, at last, it was Sophie who taught him to smile.

Very early one morning,
Sophie sat up in bed.
Something was different.
Something was coming.

Sophie tiptoed downstairs.

Her dad was looking out the window.

He put his arm around her. "Look, Sophie," he whispered.
"It's Springtime again!"

Sophie looked outside. The snow had melted. She felt a warm
feeling inside.

Right in the middle of the yard, exactly where the snowman had been, Sophie thought she could see a flower: the first flower of Spring.

She ran outside to pick it for her little brother. He had never seen Spring before.

But when she got close, Sophie found it wasn't a flower after all. It was a doll. Her own rag doll.

Sophie washed and dried the doll and dressed it in new clothes.

When they went walking, Sophie gave the rag doll to her brother.
"I don't need this anymore," she told him. "I've got you to play with now."
All through the woods, the new leaves were opening and the sun shone through the trees. It was the start of a whole new year—for Sophie and the Winter Baby.